Canice
and the Book

A short novel by

Sean Young

ISBN 978-0-9806049-0-0

First edition Published January 2009 by Fileata Fiction

ISBN 978-0-9806049-0-0

Copy sales and distribution enquiries:

Fileata Fiction
PO Box 246
Edgecliff NSW 2027
Australia
Tel 61 + 02 9332 2822
sales@fileata.com
www.fileata.com

Front cover image Brandon Cove, Co. Kerry Ireland by Sean Young.
Inside back cover - *The Cathach of Saint Columba*,
National Museum of Ireland, Dublin.
Back cover image by Sean Young and Adriene Hurst inspired by the
Kilnaruane Pillar, Bantry, West Cork, Ireland

References
Catholic Online 2008, St Canice www.catholic.org
New Advent 2008, *The Twelve Apostles of Erin*, www.newadvent.org
Baring Gould 1908, *St Cainnech*, *The Lives of the British Saints*.
Adamnan, 1998 *Life of Saint Columba*, www.fordham.edu/halsall/basis/columba-e.html
Cahil. T, 1995, *How the Irish Saved Civilisation* Sceptre,
Rutherford. E, 2004, *The Princes of Ireland*, Doubleday
Yeats. W.B, 1899 *The Song of Wandering Aengus*
Saint Patrick's Breastplate, *Liber hymnorum*, Trinity College, Dublin

imaginative fiction

For my father Fáchtna
and the people of the parish of Saint Canice,
Elizabeth Bay, Sydney, Australia

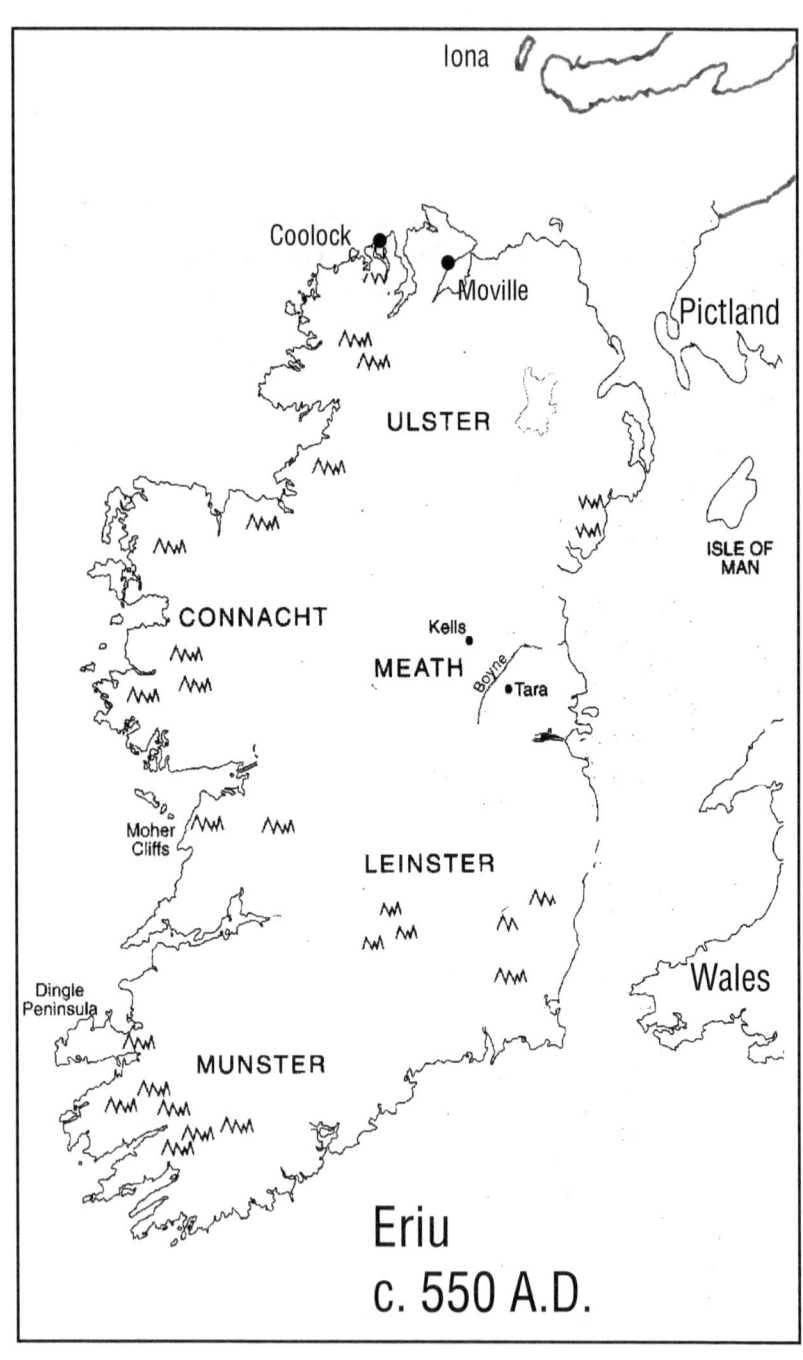

Iona

Coolock

Moville

Pictland

ULSTER

ISLE OF MAN

CONNACHT

Kells

MEATH

Boyne

Tara

Moher Cliffs

LEINSTER

Dingle Peninsula

Wales

MUNSTER

Eriu
c. 550 A.D.

1

Softly splashing, the oar touched the water as if it were stroking a girl's hair. The water dripped off the oar like fresh milk pouring from a jug, gleaming in the morning sun. Softly, the oar dipped into the water again, stroking back and forth. The sea was pensive, as if it knew a storm was coming. A rumble in the distance, and grey mist on the horizon heralded the rain and cold wind coming from the great north ocean.

Canice came back from his dream. Was it a dream? Yes, he was back, on his knees praying in his cell. He could just see the first glimmers of dawn pushing in beneath his wooden door. He started this day as he started every day, on his knees in prayer for an hour, or perhaps it was two. Most mornings he had the same transcendent dream, lost, gone as if time no longer existed. Softly the oar dipped into the water, then he came back to the world, and it was time to go to morning Mass.

Moville is a beautiful place, thought Canice. Moville lay on the western shore of Lough Foyle on the northern tip of Eriu, the island the Romans called Hibernia known today as Ireland.

Just to the north of Moville was the entrance to the sea. Rich woodland filled the country to the west. There were a few Raths, defensible farmsteads of the head men and their families, and many cattle that belonged to the great O'Neill and O'Cahan clans.

It was a wonderful feeling to be back near his home. He had been away for many years, studying and travelling. Now he was back in the region where his father Lughadh and mother Maul had raised him. His father was a bard and so, as if by osmosis, Canice had absorbed the knowledge and sensitivities that fill the soul of the Gaels. He knew the legends and songs and could recount the ancestry of the chieftains of Eriu going back many generations. He knew, too, the teachings and ways of the Druids. Although they no longer held sway over most the people, they were still the spiritual heart of the Gaels.

Canice's mother had been an early convert to the new religion. She had been baptized by Saint Patrick himself. Patrick succeeded in bringing over much of the population to Christianity by first converting influential women. Despite appearances, Eriu was a matriarchal society. The men could do nothing without the tacit approval of their women, and they loved their mothers above all else in the world.

Women were far more open to the new ideas and were able to see them as a progression of their spiritual journey rather than a threat, or so his mother told him. She said that the men's relationship with God was like a challenge. The god Lugh would perform some heroic feat, laugh at them and say, 'ha, if you can do as well as me, then you can join me in land of eternal youth.' His mother said that women could more easily understand that God, in Jesus, had come into the world, to show to us that he loved us and wanted us to join him in eternity, the world beyond time. Jesus was one of us, a friend, a nurturing generous God. He asked for nothing but love and gave unbounded love to the world.

Patrick converted the wife of a chieftain, and she invited other influential women to meet Patrick whom he also converted. Once the woman of a household changed faith, what hope was there that her soft hearted sons and husband could hold out for long? Canice's mother was one of these women, and she helped spread the new religion across Eriu.

His father had remained true to the old ways, but after he died Canice's mother encouraged him to study and become a monk. He made his way to the new monastery at Clonard. It was there that he met Columba, and he was the reason Canice had come to Moville.

Canice made the sign of the cross on his forehead and went outside into the soft morning air. It was still March and winter was not yet over. Some days, storms would come in off the ocean with a bitter cold north wind, but other days he could tell that spring was coming with a soft westerly breeze and more than a hint of warmth in the air. Today was one such day. Canice rubbed his shaven monk's head and didn't bother to pull up the hood of his habit. He wandered down the path to the church, his sandals flapping on the stones to where the rest of the monks were already gathered.

The church was in a monastery founded by the holy Finnian of Moville. Finnian had travelled to Rome and returned to Eriu with a copy of Saint Jerome's Vulgate, a very great book indeed. With this book, he had set about his evangelical mission and built his monastery.

The monks gathered in silence outside the stone church, and Finnian arrived followed by Canice's friend Columba. Finnian, Columba, and the monks proceeded into the church and started the Mass.

'God of the universe, listen to our prayers. Bend your ear to us. Let our supplications and prayers ascend to you, in the name of the one eternal God - Father, Son, and Holy Spirit,' intoned Finnian as he stood before the wooden altar. Standing beside Finnian, Columba turned the pages of the great Vulgate.

The Vulgate was a new version of the Bible, translated by Saint Jerome. Its Old Testament was the first Latin version translated directly from the Hebrew Tanakh, rather than the Greek Septuagint. Finnian had become famous for bringing this magnificent work from Rome to Eriu and many monks, including Columba, had come to read and copy it.

The monks had been trained in transcribing and illuminating the Bible and other classical books. Canice and Columba had spent years in the scriptorium at Clonard learning and practicing their skills.

When Columba heard that Finnian had brought the Vulgate to Eriu with the intention of establishing a centre at Moville, he rushed there at once. Canice, always a dreamer, stayed at Clonard. After all, he wasn't sure what his missionary calling would be, but the bold, confident Columba knew at once what he was going to do.

'This is it,' declared Columba, 'God is calling me, I will copy this great work, and with its inspiration I will evangelize the Picts.' What made Columba so sure of his mission Canice did not know as his own experience of God was much less defined.

Canice was a far gentler man than Columba; he found his spirituality in the quiet moments, away from other people, praying or contemplating a stream or watching swallows dart swiftly through the air, soaring as if on angel's wings.

Both men were now in their thirties, although Columba was a few years younger than Canice. They had been educated in Eriu and Wales and had each made separate journeys to Rome. They had both been ordained priests, but had yet to find their true calling. Because the old religion was still practised in many parts of the country, there were opportunities for evangelizing priests to set up Christian communities of their own. Canice rather enjoyed the cloistered meditative life. He liked to spend his days reading, working in the scriptorium and in prayer.

Canice was shorter than Columba, not small but with a thin frame. He always had a soft smile on his face with loving eyes. Animals loved Canice, especially dogs. The wolfhounds that belonged to the young warriors were fierce, but when they looked into Canice's soft eyes they became as gentle as tired puppies.

'Corpus Christie,' said Finnian as he placed the communion host on Canice's tongue. 'Amen,' said Canice.

When the Mass was over the monks went about their various duties. Later, Canice and Columba walked to the newly built scriptorium, Columba striding ahead in his usual ebullient manner. Canice struggled to keep up as Columba smiled and nodded at the monks they passed on their way. Although this was not a silent monastery the monks did not talk much. They concentrated on their duties and spent much time in silent contemplation.

Columba was different to the other monks. He was a well built man with a round hearty face and a beaming smile. He was the son Fedlimid, a chieftain of the great clan O'Neill. He was a great-great-grandson of Neill of the Nine Hostages, the greatest of the Irish kings who, as High King of Eriu, commanded more tribute than anyone before or after him. Columba walked and talked with the confidence of a prince, which indeed he was.

Canice could tell that Columba was meant to be an evangelist, with his expansive, generous personality matched by a deep compassion and love of Christ. He could talk with confidence and authority to any man, king, pauper or pope. Columba was about to embark on his ministry, and that was why he had called Canice to Moville.

The scriptorium was a small stone structure with benches and tables enough to seat up to eight monks. Columba was making a new book by copying parts of the Vulgate. He had been working at it for three years now and was nearly finished. Canice had only been there two months and had barely begun his version. The two monks sat down beside each other and pulled out their writing instruments from bags they carried beneath their long brown habits.

An old stern monk appeared in the doorway. He was carrying two leather bags that contained the books Canice and Columba were working on. Behind him, Finnian carried a wooden box which contained the Vulgate. They placed the bags and the box on the table. Finnian took a large key from under his habit and opened the lock on the front of the box with a clunk. He took out the Vulgate and put it down before Columba. Without speaking Finnian and the old monk departed and left them to get on with their work.

The Vulgate and the copies they were making were the most valuable possessions in the monastery. Finnian protected the book himself. Everyone assumed that he slept with it under his bed. The copies were locked in the church sacristy. The old monk was their guardian, and as he used to say, 'I am sure there are no thieves among us, but you never know if a stray Leprechaun might still be lurking around.'

They were monks and forswore violence, but Finnian and Columba were both sons of chieftains, and had spent much of their childhood riding chariots, throwing spears and swinging large shillelagh around. You could often see Finnian striding along with his spear. He wanted the local men, who were fierce warriors, to know the monastery was no easy target. Although they carefully guarded the valuable books, it was the monastery's cattle that were more likely to be taken away in the night. Cattle rustling was a favourite pastime all over Eriu among the many warriors with time on their hands and too much mead to drink.

Columba and Canice opened the leather bags and took out their books. They wrote in Latin, Columba added Gaelic text, as well. The pages of the book were made from vellum. Columba worked with a quill, but Canice preferred to use a reed. Whether a reed, or a quill, they were cured to harden, then cut at a 45-degree angle to produce a nib, split slightly lengthwise to channel the ink down from the shaft and onto the page.

They began each page with a large initial with a trumpeted end and long spiral patterns. They were highly distorted but extremely beautiful. Columba wrote the subsequent letters of the word in ever diminishing size until it was eventually the same as normal script, continuing until the end of the passage.

Columba's work was more advanced than Canice's, and he was clearly the superior scribe. Canice felt somewhat intimidated sitting beside him as he carefully drew each letter. However, Canice's copy was merely an exercise. He was not supposed to finish it. Columba had pressed him into joining him on his mission to bring the message of Christ to the Picts.

Columba had it all planned, at least in part. Perhaps it was because of his chieftain's blood, but he wasn't much of a man for organizational detail. 'God will light the way,' he beamed. He was a man with a purpose and he believed that nature would support him and provide the things he needed to complete his mission.

So far all he had actually done in preparation for his mission, was persuade some monks to join him. He had written to Canice and asked him to come to Moville. Canice had obliged but was still unsure if or when they would actually set out across the sea to their dangerous destination.

The territory of the Picts was well known to the people of Eriu. The outlying islands of Pictland could be seen off the northern coast. Indeed they had captured much territory from the Picts during the last few generations and, in fact, the Picts had migrated there from Eriu in the first place.

The Romans, who had occupied the southern part of Britain, had not conquered the highlands in the north of the island. One hundred or so years earlier they had left and since that time, the Picts had been pushing south, as the Welsh advanced east, and the clans of Eriu raided Pictland, Wales and Britain.

The Romans had brought Christianity to Britain. Saint Patrick, a Briton, and others like him had brought Christianity to Eriu. However, few people had been brave enough to try and convert the Picts. Yes, there were Pictish clans who were now Christians, but the high Pict King Bridei of Fortriu, at his base in Inverness, remained firmly in old god's time. Columba had determined that only he, of royal blood, could approach the King and bring him the good news of Christ.

Columba had forgotten some important details when planning his evangelical mission. Firstly, he did not have the blessing of his mentor and abbot, Finnian, whose monastery he was staying in. Nor had he mentioned to Finnian that he was making the book in order to take it to Pictland. Finnian assumed the book would remain at the monastery that was his life's mission. It would make a valuable addition to the library he was gathering, a priceless addition as it was a magnificent work. Indeed Finnian would frequently come to the scriptorium, and lovingly turn the pages of the unbound manuscript with delight.

In the short time Canice had been at Moville, it had become obvious to him that Columba, was about to do Finnian a terrible injustice. Canice was torn inside. He loved his friend, and he wanted to help him, but he didn't have the heart for a long evangelizing journey to wild and freezing Inverness. What he wanted was to return to the blissful routine of monastic life at Clonard. But Columba ureged him on saying, 'You're the only one I can trust Canice. God trusts you, he listens to you. Have a word with God, will you Canice. He will light the way.'

'Columba, your work is beautiful, so much better than mine.'

Columba laughed and said, 'Canice, your work is beautiful, too. But this book is special. It's my grand opus, the best I will ever do.'

'I am sure you will find many opportunities to do better. Finnian holds you in high regard,' said Canice, tugging at Columba's conscience.

'Finnian, ah well, there is small a problem there,' Columba said sheepishly.

'So you've told him of your wish to travel then, to go to Pictland?'

'Yes, I told him all right.'

'What did he say?'

'He said I was to stay and finish the book. He has taken a shine to it. He thinks it is very special, too, and wants it for his new library he intends to build here at the monastery. So I am to stay put and do as I am told,' replied Columba with obvious frustration.

Canice chirped hopefully, ' Ah, he is a great man Finnian, a great teacher and very holy. We could do a lot worse than be here with him.'

'Yes, a great teacher, but I want to be a great teacher, too. I've studied for years, both here and in Clonard. I have been to Rome, and I have a different path in mind.'

'The Picts,' sighed Canice'

'Someone has to convert them. They can't stay in old god's time forever.'

'Why you, Columba?'

'It's my calling, I can feel it in my heart. I am going soon, and I am taking my book with me.'

'You can't take the book, Columba. Sure, Finnian will kill ye!'

Finian walked in, looked over Columba's shoulder and smiled at the book. 'Ah Columba, such beauty flows from your nib. This book will be my great gift to the Church and people of Ulster. It will shine as bright as the Star of the Sea.' Finnian walked out again.

'MY gift to the Church! This book has taken me years, it's mine! I'm going - going soon. WITH MY BOOK!' Columba thundered.

2

Canice wasn't aware of the cold night air or the wind coming off the north ocean. He ended every day as he began it, kneeling deep in prayer. He thanked God for all that had taken place during the day, offered his life to him and asked for direction so that he might be of some use to the people around him. He then began to recite to himself a long list of people he had to pray for; his parents and siblings, holy Finnian, the Pope, the O'Neill clan, Columba, the smith back at Clonard who wanted a child, the woman with the sick husband, all the people of Eriu, the Welsh, the Picts. The list was long and always growing longer.

The people around him soon recognised that he was praying for them. They would mention someone's name and Canice would say, 'I pray for him every day.' Indeed, at any time that Canice was not performing his monk's duties he would be praying. If he walked into the Raths near Clonard, people would shout out requests for him to pray for sick or dead relatives. If a couple wanted a child they would ask Canice to pray for them. If a cattleman wanted fertile cows, he would ask Canice to put in a good word with, 'yer man in heaven', for him. So Canice prayed for everyone, every morning and every night and in between times, too.

When he was praying, after a while, he never knew how long, it was as if he had ceased to exist and as if the world and time stood still. His absence might only have lasted an instant, but it would seem like an eternity - eternity without time. When he came back, he simply knew that he had been gone and that now he was back. He would seep into a glowing reverie with sweet happiness oozing from every pore of his being. His eyes still shut, his mind would be at sea, rowing, with the delicious sound of the waves, the spray, the oar dipping in and out of the water. The water slipping off his oar as if it were milk pouring slowly from a jug, the sunshine glistening on the crest of the waves, the wind in his face, the smell of the sea, bliss.

A loud noise shattered Canice's peace. He heard shouting, running and torches sent light flashing under the door into his cell.

'Quick get him, over here.'

'Yeaooo, I've broken my toe, you cursed wretch! Wait till I get ye.'

Columba crashed in and closed the door behind him.

'Columba, what's going on?'

Columba whispered, 'I'm going. I've got my book, but Finnian caught me. I tried to get away, but he set them on me. Oh my God, I struck one of them. By Christ, I think I might've killed him!'

'What, what now?!'

'Canice, I'm going, but I can't risk taking the book. If they catch me, I'll have lost it. Here, you take it!' He thrust the leather bag holding the book into Canice's hands. 'Quick, come with me.'

He dragged Canice by the hand out into the night. The monks and Finnian were searching for Columba down the hill towards the sea. They could see their torches flashing, running back and forth, and hear their shouts. 'You cursed wretch,' but the sounds were further away now. Columba dragged Canice up the hill into the woods. They ran and ran through the darkness and wind. When they were in the thick of the woods, Canice could go no further. He fell and cried, 'Columba, stop, I have to catch my breath.' Both men gasped for air, and Canice thought his heart would explode.

When they had calmed down, Columba said, 'Canice, I know I can trust you. I can't trust anybody else. You have the book. Meet me at Coolock. I am going south first to get the monks who said they will come with me. I'll meet you there, and we'll row over to Pictland.'

'Columba, I have never been to Coolock before. How far away is it? I've no food, I must go back.'

Columba backed away into the night. 'You have the book, Canice. I can trust you, and you're the only one I can trust. Besides, if Finnian finds you with that book he'll make cat's meat out of you! Coolock is where the northwestern shore of Lough Swilly meets the sea. Head west until you reach the Lough, then follow the shoreline to the sea, and you'll find Coolock.'

'Columba, good God, don't leave me. I'm not a strong man like you. I've no skills for the wilds. I've spent so many years reading and praying, sure, you can't leave me.'

'Have a word with God. He'll listen to you. He'll help you find

Coolock. Just go west along the coast, you can't miss it. God will light the way. See you soon, my friend.' Columba disappeared into the forest.

Canice heard the monks from the monastery coming towards him. Torches flashed, dogs barked and Finnian shrieked, 'Columba, come out you divil! I'll make cat's meat out of you! I want my book, and you've killed a man!'

Canice stumbled away up into the woods. **Eventually, he could hear no more noise, so he curled up exhausted, in his habit and fell into a desperate sleep.**

It was still dark when Canice awoke. He kept his eyes shut. He was cold, but that was not new to him. As he did every morning, he started to pray.

I arise today through a mighty strength, the invocation of the Trinity,
Through the belief in the threeness,
Through confession of the oneness,
Of the Creator of Creation.
I arise today through the strength of Christ's birth with his baptism,
Through the strength of his crucifixion with his burial,
Through the strength of his resurrection with his ascension,
Through the strength of his descent for the judgment of Doom...

As the words of his silent prayer echoed in his mind, he remembered the events of the night before. He opened one eye and realised, I'm not in my cell. Where the devil am I? He jumped up with a start, and the entire episode came back to him. He looked down, and saw the leather pouch with Columba's book in it. Dear God, he thought, what should I do? For the first time in many years, he didn't continue his prayers. Not the sick, or the dead, or the Welsh, or the man whose cows weren't producing were remembered that morning.

Perplexed, he began to walk, not knowing which way to go. After a time, the sun rose above the horizon and shone through the trees, and he knew he was travelling west. He had never heard of Coolock until Columba mentioned it. But he knew that Moville was on the western shore of Lough Foyle and that the lough poured into the sea to the north.

His family were from the other side of the lough near the eastern shore. His parents were both dead now, but he had other relatives over there. To find them, he would have to follow the shore of the lough to the south, then cross the river Foyle. On foot, it was a journey of some days. If Finnian intended to look for him, he would certainly try and intercept him at the ford. Columba said he should follow the shore of Lough Swilly to find Coolock. At least it was in the opposite direction, so maybe Columba wasn't a complete idiot after all.

Canice mulled over the situation as he walked. Columba is in the wrong, but Finnian will forgive him. This can only be resolved by Columba asking forgiveness and returning the book. If I return the book to Finnian, Columba will think I've betrayed him, and Finnian will have no need to forgive Columba as he will have the prized book. Columba may do something crazy like trying to steal his book back again.

No, the only thing to do is head west and try to find Coolock before I die of exposure. Columba will have calmed down by the time I get there, presuming Finnian hasn't caught him and fed him to his cats. Then I can persuade Columba to make amends with Finnian. So that became Canice's plan.

The country he passed through was beautiful but wild. Somehow he had stumbled away from any tracks or cattle grazing areas and was in an oak forest. After walking most of the day, he had seen no signs of habitation or any human activity. He knew that this was where the druids used to send their young novices for spiritual training and to learn about the forest plants and their medicinal properties. The druids were the healers as well as the spiritual guides of the people.

He was taught as a child that this area was sacred to the Tuatha Dé Danann, the people native to Eriu before the Sons of Mill had arrived by sea. The new arrivals struck a bargain with the goddess Eriu whereby they could inhabit the area above the ground, while the Tuatha Dé Danann would keep the area underground. So it was that Eriu allowed the Sons of Mill, the Gaels, to come ashore and inhabit the island.

An essential part of the bargain with Eriu was that the Gaels should leave the Tuatha Dé Danann in peace. There were areas all over Eriu where the 'Little People', as they were known, were fabled to live. People did their best to leave those places in peace, because they knew that if you unwittingly disturbed a Lish, the mounds that marked the entrances to the underground world of the Little People, then 'your cows won't milk, your women won't produce, your men will wander the lonely shores forever like the sad curlew and never find a mate'.

Canice knew these things because he was a Gael. He was especially familiar with the tales of the Little People because he was the son of a bard. The bards were the keepers of the lore, the songs and the rich oral culture that was passed down through the generations. Canice, in fact, was a bard himself, but he had become a Christian monk. Hence he rejected the stories of Eriu, Lugh and the pantheon of gods that everyone believed in before Saint Patrick. At least, on the surface he rejected the old beliefs.

He certainly accepted the divinity of Christ and had dedicated his life to following his teachings. However, in his heart, under his skin, he knew that the old stories were also true, that Eriu was the beautiful mother Goddess. He accepted that Eriu, her husband Mac Griene, Lugh the dashing God king and Mamannan Mac Lir God of the Sea, were real to his ancestors. He beleived that, in truth, they were still real, and that the Trinity of God the Father, Son and Holy Spirit was but another human description of the same omnipresent God. For, if there were only one true God, how could there be two? How could humans, mere mortals, comprehend omnipresence and omnipotence?

He believed that God was manifest in all things and transcended time and life. Indeed, existence itself is God made manifest. These truths Canice understood, and he felt no conflict in both being both a follower of Christ and a Gael. He believed that God sent us his son Jesus to show us the way to achieve unity with him. Like a shepherd appearing on the hill side, beckoning the sheep towards Him, 'Come my little ones, come over here, this is the way.'

Night fell, and although he was cold, tired and thirsty, he fell to his knees and made his nightly prayers. The next morning, he was woken by the pitter patter of cold, icy rain on his habit. He opened his eyes in the darkness and stretched his hand out into the frigid air. An icy slush was falling on him through the trees. Well, at least he wouldn't die of thirst. How far was it to the coastline, he wondered? No point lying here in the sleet, I had better get going, he thought.

As the day went on, he grew weaker. Spring had barely arrived, so there were no berries to eat yet. He should have been more knowledgeable about the edible forest vegetation, but since his early teens he had studied the Bible and not the woods. The rain continued all day. He knew by the wind roaring through the trees that a heavy storm was descending from the north ocean. In the summer and autumn months, the weather came from the west and south and blessed Eriu with pleasant moist, warm winds for much of the time. But in winter and spring, storms would come from further north, icy cold and brutal.

He felt weak and hungry but continued on his way. The days started to follow a terrible routine. Cold and wet, he would walk all day long until darkness halted his progress. He would fall into a shivering sleep, glimpsing the silver moon piercing through the clouds. He didn't have the strength for prayers any longer, and would be awakened by freezing rain, to stumble up and continue on his way. This continued for several days. He wasn't sure how many.

One morning, he walked across the crest of a hill to the edge of the woodlands and into open country. He came in sight of Lough Swilly and clambered over rocks and brooks until he was near the mouth of a small river by the shore, and could go no further.

He collapsed to his knees and with all his remaining strength he prayed aloud. 'Dear Father in heaven, I have sinned. Help me, forgive me. I am lost, in a maelstrom, I am afraid, and I have no hope. I am weak and torn. I love you, my God, and I beg for your mercy.'

He stared out across the water and, slowly, a vision appeared through the waves, a woman dressed in flowing robes with emerald green eyes. She had a star above her head and smiled at him. He didn't know if he were dying or dreaming. He was transfixed by the beautiful vision before him, with her long brown hair and piercing eyes that were a rich deep green, but so bright that their gaze radiated out from her round, softly smiling face.

She spoke to him. 'Canice, why are you afraid?'

'I have sinned. I have turned away from God and lost him.'

'Canice, you may have lost God, but God has not lost you. Do not fear, are not two sparrows sold for a sip of water? Yet not one of them will fall to the ground away from the Father. Even the hairs on your head are counted.' Canice felt his bald monk's head. 'So do not be afraid, surely you are as valuable as many sparrows,' she said with a laughing smile, her hair waving in the wind.

Her eyes reached into him like tendril beams from the bright sun. He felt a rush of joy and a warm sensation as if he were a boy wrapped in his mother's arms. It was as if his whole life, past, present and that to come were happening all at once. The woman laughed and slowly faded away back into the waves.

He awoke as if from a trance. Suddenly, his head felt clear. He felt a calmness and resolution. He was no longer afraid. The weather had turned soft with a light breeze and warming sunshine on his back. He noticed a bird sitting in a tree on the bank of the river just beside him. It had a sprig of berries in its beak. The bird dropped the berries and Canice picked them up and ate them. They were red, sweet and juicy. After so long without eating, they were the most delicious food he had ever tasted.

The bird twittered and fluttered and seemed to want Canice to follow him. So Canice followed the little bird back up the river deep into the forest. After a time, they came to a clearing in the middle of which was large bush laden with beautiful red berries. Canice ran to the bush and helped himself to the fruit. The bird watched him, and he saw that there were many birds sitting in the bush looking at him. He supposed that they would not mind if he took some of the delicious berries. So he ate, and his spirits improved. It was as if he had been away for a long time, but now was home.

A stag stood at the edge of the clearing watching him, and he heard a crunching sound as a cow emerged from the undergrowth. She was laden with milk and mooed at him. Like everyone in Eriu, he had been brought up surrounded by cows, so he knew how to milk one. He gently pulled her teat and warm milk spurted into his hands, which he lapped up. Canice spent the day by his berry bush eating and drinking milk in the company of the birds, the stag and the cow.

The next day he awoke much refreshed. A bird flew up to him with a long blade of tussock grass in its beak. He took the grass, picked a berry and threaded the grass through it. He made little a rod out of a twig. He and carried it to the stream and dangled the berry in the water. In a flash, a little silver trout appeared to jump onto his berry, and he pulled it out of the water and smiled. It was an old trick he had learned as a boy. He and his brothers spent many days playing by the streams that fed into Lough Foyle. That time seemed so long ago now. He looked at the little silver fish flapping in his hand and felt so much empathy for the poor creature that he gently placed it back in the water. He had plenty of berries to eat and milk to drink anyway.

He spent several days sitting by the bush and stream with the animals, regaining his strength. One day, all the fruit from the tree was gone, and so he left the clearing, after saying goodbye to the stag and the cow. The birds made a cacophony of song as a farewell, and he continued on his journey.

He went back to the coast and continued around the Lough as Columba had told him to do. After another two days, he began to see signs of habitation, a path, smoke and a house. He followed the path and after a while, he saw a man walking towards him from the opposite direction.

'Fine day,' said the man.

'Sure it is, a beautiful day, and would Coolock be anywhere near here?' Canice asked.

'You'll not go wrong if you keep going the way you are,' the fellow answered.

'Would it be very far?'

'I would be lying if I said I could not get there myself before I had passed too much time on my journey between the immensities.'

'The immensities?'

'Of birth and death,' said the man.

Didn't the people of Eriu love to talk, they were all philosophers and poets, thought Canice. 'I don't suppose you would be able to take me to Coolock. I've been on an arduous journey.'

'I'll keep going my way, and you keep going your way, and we may meet on the path of God again some day. May the road rise up to meet you. Good day to you, holy monk.'

With that, the man continued on his way and Canice kept going, too. At day's end, he saw a Rath by the sea with several monk's cells around it. His heart jumped – surely, this must be Coolock. He continued down the path and saw a large monk with his back to him standing characteristically with his hands on his hips. Could it be Columba? The monk turned around and caught sight of Canice. With a beaming smile, he ran towards him.

'Canice, I can't believe it. I thought I had lost you. I thought I had killed two men!'

'Thank God, I am alright, Columba. Thank God, and here is your book!' Canice pulled out the book from his habit and gave it to his friend.

Columba unwrapped it and smiled. 'Now, we can all go and convert the Picts!' He put his arms around Canice, and they walked together into the Rath.

3

Columba had gathered four other monks with him at Coolock. 'Men of God, this is Canice who I told you so much about. Let us drop to our knees and thank the Lord for bringing him safely to us. Oh, and for my book, as well. Thank you, Canice, for keeping it safe for me. Let us pray.' The monks formed a circle, fell to their knees and prayed together.

The Rath belonged to Colman and his extended family. He lived in the main building with his wife and children. The surrounding countryside was dotted with other dwellings where his brothers and cousins lived. In those times, many monks would spend at least some period in the remotest areas of the country. Some of them even went to offshore islands and climbed cliffs to be as isolated as possible. A few years earlier, a group of monks that Columba knew came to this area to find seclusion and pray. Colman, whose family had been converted when he was a child, let the monks build a small stone church and several earth and wattle huts or cells stay in. The monks would come and go, staying only a while. This was how Columba had come to know about Coolock and why he had chosen it as the starting point for his journey. That night, they ate with Colman and his family, and Canice was allocated a cell to sleep in up the hill.

Canice awoke in the morning with his eyes still closed, and he began to pray to himself as he did every morning.

I arise today, through a mighty strength, the invocation of the Trinity,
Through the belief in the threeness,
Through confession of the oneness
Of the Creator of Creation...

He completed his prayers and opened the door of the little thatched, honeycomb-like cell and went out into the dawn. The Rath of Coolock was situated on a gentle slope leading down to a small natural harbour. His cell was high enough above the sea to give him a magnificent view of the surrounding coastline. To the south there were hills and coves sheltering sandy beaches. Waves crashed against cliffs on headlands far down the coast. To the north, a bay stretched around to the east. Looking east, he could see the first rays of the sun shining with little fingers, illuminating the topmost hills then pouring down the hillsides to the water of the bay. The peninsulas and islands in the bay looked golden and then green in the morning sun, a green like the eyes of the woman he saw in his vision.

This was surely the most beautiful shoreline he had ever seen. Watching the scene unfold was like listening to a harp playing, each pluck of the string wrenching tears of love and sweet sadness from his heart. He thought of his vision and the beautiful woman whom he supposed to be Eriu herself, come to rescue him.

The little church had been built a bit down the hill. The Rath was a bit further on from the church, and the harbour was at the bottom of the hill. He could see a large currach on the shore, the boat that Columba had obtained for the journey across the sea.

The other monks were gathering down by the church for morning Mass, and Canice wandered down to meet them, his sandals flip flopping on the stones.

The monks all nodded in silence to each other, Columba arrived, and they all proceeded inside. Around the church grew several trees and as Canice approached, birds fluttered into the branches and twittered at each other. Once inside Columba started to say Mass.

'Nomine Patris, et Filii, et Spiritus Sancti'

Chirup, chiurp, cheep, cheep, CHIURP CHIURP CHEEP CHEEP!

The sound of the birds was overwhelming, and Columba could barely hear himself. He turned and looked at Canice. 'Will you not go have a word with them?'

Canice hurried outside and went up to one of the trees. He murmured to the birds and smiled. They began to quieten down, and he went inside again. Columba continued with the Mass, and when it came time to read, he opened his book. The still unbound pages shone brightly in the little room. The other monks had never seen the book before and gasped at the beauty of it. Columba turned over the leaves seeking a suitable a passage to read out loud.

After Mass, the monks went down to prepare for the voyage. The boat was a sea going currach used for offshore fishing. It was long enough to hold eight oarsmen with a depth of roughly half a body length. It had an internal wooden frame and was covered in stretched cow leather. There were five wooden benches laid across the currach for the oarsmen to sit on. The bow of the boat turned up in a graceful curve, and the stern was square. The bottom of the craft was a flat u shape with no protrusions. The navigator sat in the stern and put a broad paddle into the water and lashed it to a post in the aft gunwale. This would be used as a rudder while the oarsmen with their backs to the bow would row one, man per oar.

The local people had made the boat themselves, and as Colman said, 'If Eriu and Mamannan Mac Lir will allow it, this little currach will take you all over the world.'

The monks loaded skins full of water and bags of oats and barley into the boat. They carefully placed skins of mead into the very bottom - they did not want that cargo in particular to be washed overboard. The monks were merry laughing, and teasing each other.

'Aongus, will you be able to heave your fat behind into this delicate craft, do you think?'

'You look after your own oar and leave my behind to me, Fáchtna!'

One of the monks tapped his fist on the leather side of the boat to make a loud drumming sound. Then another monk drummed. Soon the four monks Columba and Canice were singing a hearty tune to the accompaniment of several hands drumming the boat, and they all fell about laughing.

A man and woman came up to the gathering and asked Columba. 'Holy monk, could we trouble to ask your help in a small matter? We've heard that one of you has a way with the little creatures.'

Canice thought, 'Ah, they will want me to pray for them. I'll be happy to add them to my list.'

They took Columba to one side and whispered earnestly to him. 'Come on, Canice,' said Columba after hearing what they had to say. 'We'll take the little currach over here and go out to the island in the bay. These folks have a job for you.'

Canice and Columba got into a two-man currach and followed the couple as they rowed out to one of the small islands in the bay a short distance from the harbour.

When they arrived at the island, they could see mice running everywhere. As they walked up the sandy beach, they were almost tripping over them. The woman said to Canice, 'Will you have a word with them, holy monk? They're eating everything.'

Canice walked off up into the fields behind the beach. Columba and the couple watched as he talked to the mice that crowded around his legs. After a few minutes, Canice came back and smiled. The mice gathered on the beach in huge numbers, and forming a long line, they pushed into the water and began to swim. They watched as the mice swam across the water to the mainland and emerged on the other shore and dispersed.

'Thank you, holy monk. Don't you have a way with the little ones.'

Columba laughed out loud in amazement at Canice and gave him a wry look. The two monks got back into the currach and rowed back to the harbour.

On the way Canice asked, 'Are you sure about the voyage to Pictland, Columba?'

'I am. The weather looks soft.'

'What about the book?'

'What about it?'

'You can't keep the book, Columba!'

'Why not? It's mine'

'You're a priest, Columba. You don't own anything, not even the book.'

'Well, whose book is it then, Finnian's? I made the book. Finnian said I could make it. I've spent years working on it. Why does he want it anyway? It's mine!'

The oars cut the water, not softly but harshly, slapping, splashing as the two men rowed on in silence.

'Here you are, running off to Pictland, no community, in disgrace.'

'We'll see. I think this is God's way of telling me to go and bring the good news to the Picts.'

'Are you not afraid?'

'They are fierce, it's true, but God will protect us. You have a word with God for us, Canice. He'll listen to you.'

Row, row, slap splash.

'I've known you a long time, brother, but I can't go with you.'

'You have to come with us, Canice. You've no choice. You don't understand. Finnian will never take you back.'

'All because of the book, the unfinished book.'

'I am going to use that book to convert the Picts. That is why I made it, to show them the glory of God and teach them the Bible.'

'You could have taken another book and had Finnian's blessing.'

'He prefers my copy of the book, that's what it is. My book is better than his, and he's jealous! Finnian thinks it's magic. Books are the new magic.'

'Don't go, Columba. It's too dangerous. Just give the book back and make up with Finnian. The people here need you, Columba.'

'They have Finnian. The Picts need me, and they need you as well Canice. They are people, too, and they need your help.'

'I'm no good with people, Columba. It's the animals that love me.'

'You're close to creatures because they are close to God. But it's the people who need you! You must help them get close to God.'

'They won't listen to me. God won't listen to me, either.'

'You must treat people like you treat the creatures. Like children of God, not children of men. Then they will understand you. You have to come with me. The alternative is the wrath of Finnian.'

'You're as stubborn as Balor with the belly of a Fir Bolug, Columba!'

'Canice, you came to Moville when I asked you. You kept the book safe for me. Now, you must complete your mission. I need you to help me convert the Picts.'

'All right, I'll come with you then. What else can I do?'

With a splash and clunk, the boat arrived at the shore. Canice and Columba jumped out of the boat, glared at each other in anger and marched off in opposite directions.

They were to set off the next morning. The weather looked fine, but you could never be sure how long it would last. The weather changed like the 'whim of a girl', the locals said. One moment the sea would be like a mirror, the next a raging torrent. Still, it looked fine now, and as the sunset and evening came, the monks gathered at the main building of the Rath. Colman was giving them a farewell party.

The people from Colman's extended family had come from their houses dotted around Coolock. Colman had a well built single story house made of mud and wattle. It had one large room with a fireplace and large hearth at one end. The hearth was the main focus of the house and his wife could almost always be found working there, chopping vegetables or curdling milk from the many cows that Colman had, or cooking barley or fish. He had seven children ranging from two to twenty two years old.

His various cousins and brothers, their spouses and children that made up his extended family, filled the room and spilled out into the courtyard.

The courtyard was large and circled the house. At its edges, earth had been heaped to form a low wall and on top of that was a fence made of wattle. Cows, pigs and ducks from the farm had gathered within the walls. where the family would bring them for milking or feeding. Now, with all the party goers crowding in the animals were running and flapping all over. Colman's young children were chasing them and trying to shoo them out of the yard.

The men were tucking into the mead, slapping each other on their backs and guffawing. Several of the women had formed a circle and were singing a round song. One woman sang a phrase and then the woman beside her would sing the next and so on around it went. The young girls were dancing in the middle, their arms at their sides and their hair flying in all directions.

This chaos nearly overwhelmed Canice. It reminded him of the parties at home when he was young. But for so long now he had lived the quiet life, just nodding hello to his fellow monks. Amid this confusion of shouting, singing and quacking he thought he might faint. A piper arrived, playing a merry tune. The whole crowd cheered and jumped up in a wild dance. Canice was lifted with them, a pretty young woman on one arm and a burly farmer with a jug of mead in his hand on his other arm, flying around the yard with everyone else, and ducks landing on their heads.

Singing, dancing, and drinking continued on into the evening until finally, the party grew more peaceful. Groups of people stood around telling each other how many cattle they had and recounting tales of adventure. Faces were illuminated by the hearth fire. Smiling eyes stared into the flickering flames as they listened to their cousins tell stories they had heard a hundred times before.

The room quietened to a hush as a small man sitting on a stool in a corner of the house declared, 'Perhaps I will play something for ye now.'

Colman whispered, 'Ah, the great bard himself is going to play.'

They turned to the little man. His eyes were closed, but opened occasionally to show pure white eyeballs, for he was blind. He had a little harp on his knee. After allowing the crowd to settle completely, he paused for effect and plucked his harp sweetly.

No one at Coolock had ever heard the great bard before, but they knew his reputation. He had played all across Eriu for the chieftains and at the annual religious festivals. Bards spent much of their time crisscrossing the country, and served a variety of functions. They would be summoned to an area to recount in detail the lineage of the local clan, for example, to assist in settling grazing disputes and the like. They would also perform at weddings and gatherings, both Christian and old Gods' festivals. At other times, bards would go on journeys just to satisfy their own curiosity. They would be sure to find employment along the way.

On such a journey, the great bard had found his way to Coolock, riding a horse with a teenage boy to help him. Canice's father was a bard and had he lived longer, Canice would have travelled more with him. Canice remembered one occasion when his father proclaimed, 'I am off now to wander the land and learn the secrets of our beloved island. Now Canice, you stay here and look after your mother. But don't forget me! I'll be back before you're married.'

The bard now played the sweetest, saddest melody the gathering had ever heard. The listeners were carried off in their own dreams and memories. For Canice, it felt as if he were flying across the sea like a gull, swooping along the cliffs down to the water and back up to the clouds. His emotions soared from intense joy and boundless love to sweet sorrow such as he had felt when his father departed for the last time, then back down again, to land, at the Rath of Colman, by the fire.

When the beautiful sound stopped, everyone was lost in a reverie. Some had tears on their cheeks. The young snuggled to their mothers breasts. Columba's and the monk's eyes were glazed as they stared into the flames.

4

The next morning, Canice awoke, his still eyes closed. *I arise today through a mighty strength, the invocation of the Trinity…*He went out into the dawn and took in the sweeping views. It was a magnificent day. The sun burst its first tendrils across the land and into the sea. He had no possessions with him, having left everything back at Moville, so he simply glanced back at the cell that had been his home for such a short while and with resignation started down the path to the harbour.

Columba and the monks were already there, busily getting onto the currach, though looking a bit sheepish and sallow after the antics of the night before. Canice approached and clasped his two hands onto the side of the boat. He was about to clamber aboard, when Columba put his hand on his shoulder.

'Take this, Canice.' He handed him the book and his writing tools. 'It's our book now. I want you to stay and finish it.'

'But how will the book help you if I have it?'

'Finish it, look after it, and you can bring it over to Pictland when I have established my church.'

Columba and the monks climbed into the currach, and Colman and his cousins shoved the boat away from the shore. Columba gazed at Canice with a broad, benevolent smile. He took up his seat at the aft of the boat, dipped his steering oar into the water and encouraged his hungover monks. 'Come on now, lads. We're off to do God's work. You'll feel better once we get going.'

The monks looked unconvinced but slowly gathered their senses and together dipped their oars into the water. Soon, as if no time had passed, Canice, Colman and his family were left standing silently on the shore, the currach out of sight at sea. With nothing more to do, they all shrugged and wandered off.

Well how about that, thought Canice. He rubbed his bald monk's head and walked slowly up the hill. He sat down by his cell and thought, Lucky Columba, he knows what his calling is. What's mine? I know I want to be a priest and a monk. I have to do something useful for the people. I can't just chase mice away. What should I do now? Maybe I should go back to Clonard. What am I to do with the book? If I am found with it, Finnian will go mad. He sighed and looked out to sea. Could he see the currach? No, but he did see the slightest bit of grey cloud on the horizon in the west.

Anyway, perhaps I should have a look at this book. He took the book and writing tools and sat on a stone wall just next to his cell. He placed the book flat on the wall and opened to the last page that had been worked on. It was the Psalm *Trust in God Alone*. The text of the Psalm had been written,

… who made heaven and earth and the sea and all that is in them…

Yes all that is in the sea. God, look after Columba, he prayed.

He took out the box of Columba's writing instruments and opened it. He rolled Columba's quill in his finger and thumb. Although the text was there, the embellishments were not complete, but he could see what Columba had been doing and where he had left off. He felt a desire to start drawing, but he was not in a scriptorium, and he lacked a proper place to work on the page. Then he saw a stag in the bushes near him. He beckoned the stag over and the animal bowed his head presenting his antlers. Canice placed the unfinished page in the stag's antlers. He took out the black oak gall ink and dipped his quill in and loaded it with ink. He then touched the velum with the quill and started to complete a series of swirling spirals that Columba had begun.

The day passed, and Canice let the stag go back to the woods. As the sun was setting, the dark clouds had moved in from the west were nearly overhead. Then he heard a rumble and saw a flash of lightning. 'Yes, God, please look after Columba.'

He ate an evening meal down at the Rath. Colman's little son Fionbarr offered Canice some left over mead. Canice grimaced at the thought, and patted the boy on the head as he declined. He went back to his cell and said his evening prayers as always. He included the mice he had asked to leave the little island and, of course, Columba and the monks in his list of requests to God.

He was sound asleep when he heard it. 'Canice, Canice, will ye have a word with God for us, we need it now!' He awoke with a start. With a terrible feeling of dread, he got up and rushed outside. It was not raining, but there were no stars, and a howling gale punished the trees and churned the sea.

He ran down the path to the church, his sandals flip flopping furiously on the stones. In the dark, one of his sandals fell off, but he didn't hesitate. He rushed into the church and, falling to his knees, sank into deep prayer.

At sea, the face of Columba peered through the darkness. Craaak! The sky lit up bright blue for an instant and lightning danced across the sky. 'Hold on, men!' Columba shouted. The rain came down in sheets and, the boat went up bow-first on a wave, up, up, up. Then it seemed to stop until the bow plummeted as if it were falling into a gigantic hole, and the boat dropped down, down. The monks could do nothing except huddle in the bottom of the currach and hold on to the wooden struts.

Currachs were fine vessels in calm water. They could be fun in surf, crashing though the waves to shore, but they were unstable and prone to skid over the water, turning circles requiring a skilled helmsman to steady the craft. Burly Columba was a skilled boatman, but this was a full-fledged storm and all he could do was hold on. Another wave surged, and the boat rose up again, still higher. This time Columba could not control the currach and, as it reached the top of the wave, it spun around like a top and slipped down the wave backwards. Water filled the boat and the men were certain they were doomed.

Columba, his eyes shining bright in he darkness urged them, 'You have to start rowing again. It's the only way. I can't steer her otherwise.' The drenched monks struggled to take their places and find their oars as a gigantic wave crashed straight over them. They bailed the boat again and, huddled together not knowing what to do. They felt the boat going up the side of another wave and were blinded streak of lightening followed almost instantaneously by a huge thunder clap.

The monks were terrified, but Columba smiled down at them in the bottom of the boat and said, 'Don't worry men. Canice is praying for us right now. He only has one shoe on. God will listen to him.' Columba's smile shone through the rain.

Colman's little boy woke before dawn as always. He whistled the tune the bard had played the night before last and wandered up the hill, to find the ducks and herd them with his stick back to the Rath to be fed. He saw a sandal on the foot path. 'That's not mine, is it me da's?' Then he remembered the silly monk who looked so funny with a duck sitting on his head. He took the sandal up to Canice's cell, but he wasn't there. He went to look for him in the church.

He entered slowly and saw Canice on his knees, his hands clasped together in front of him, his head bowed. His feet were sticking out behind him, and he only had one sandal on. The young boy tiptoed up to him and slipped the sandal onto his foot. What was the silly monk doing? He sat down beside Canice and stared up at his face.

Softly splashing, the oar touched the water as if it were stroking a girl's hair. Softly, the oar dipped into the water again, stroking back and forth. The sea was pensive, as if it knew a storm was coming. A rumble in the distance, and grey mist on the horizon heralded the rain and cold wind coming from the great north ocean.

Canice felt a slight tug. Like a single drop of rain, falling on his skin. It was enough to bring him back. His dream began to fade. Where was he? Oh yes, the storm, Columba and the monks in danger, in the waves. He had asked God to help them. How long had he been there? Hadn't he lost a shoe? He cracked open one eye and saw the face of a puzzled little boy staring back at him. He opened both eyes. Yes, it was the fair headed boy, Fionbarr. He patted him on the head and smiled. He looked over his shoulder and saw he had two shoes on after all. No matter. He took the boy by the hand and together they walked outside.

He looked south to the hills and coves sheltering sandy beaches. Waves crashed against cliffs on headlands far down the coast. To the north, the bay that stretched around to the east looked glassy calm. Looking east, he could see the first rays of the sun shining with little fingers illuminating the topmost hills then, pouring down the hillsides to the water of the bay. The peninsulas and islands in the bay looked golden and then green in the morning sun, a green like the eyes of the woman he saw in his vision. He thought of his vision, the beautiful woman, Eriu herself, who had come to rescue him.

Slowly the oars cut the water, dipping in, up and back. Softly splashing, the water dripped off the oars like fresh milk pouring from a jug, gleaming in the morning sun. The monks fixed on Columba's broad, smiling face as they rowed, and felt secure after the fear and tension of the night before. They were safe now - certain to reach the distant shore they could see in the dawn light.

XXXXXXX

Who were Canice and Columba?

Saint Canice (known in Ireland as Canice, and as Canice in Scotland) was an Irish priest, missionary and monastic founder. He was a man of great virtue, eloquence and learning. Known in Scotland as Saint Canice, he was closely associated with Saint Columba and helped him in his missionary work in Pictland, modern day Scotland. He was born in 515 at Glengiven, County Derry, and died in 600.

Canice's father Lughadh was a distinguished bard, a highly trained professional poet and keeper of Gaelic oral tradition.

In 5th and 6th century Ireland after the collapse of the druidic tradition, the study of Latin and Christian theology in monasteries flourished. In 543 Canice became a pupil at the monastic school at Clonard, where many important figures in the history of Irish Christianity studied. It was at Clonard that Canice became a close friend and companion of Saint Columba.

Canice founded the monastery and Abbey of Aghaboe, which eventually moved to modern day Kilkenny, translated from Irish as the Church of Canice, the city and county named after him.

Columba was a great-great-grandson of Niall of the Nine Hostages, high king of Ireland during the 4th century. He was born in 521 and died in 597.

Columba had a quarrel with Saint Finnian of Moville over a book. He had copied a manuscript at Finnian's scriptorium, intending to keep it. However, Finnian disputed his right to the book. The quarrel led Columba to voyage to Scotland where he was granted land on the island of Iona off the west coast.

There he founded a monastery that became the centre of his evangelizing mission to the Picts and a school for missionaries. People travelled from all over western Europe to study under him.

He was a skilled scribe and a renowned man of letters. It is believed that he made 300 books with his own hand, two of which, *The Book of Durrow* and a psalter called *The Cathach*, are said to have been preserved to the present time.

Columba was a leading figure in the Celtic church and was instrumental in bringing a revival of Christianity to Western Europe after the fall of the Roman Empire.

The Cathach of Saint Columba

An early seventh century Irish Psalter. Traditionally associated
with Columba and beleived to be a copy he made of a book
loaned to him by Saint Finnian.

Sean De Siun spent his early years in Australia before moving to London in the early 1970s.

His written works include non fiction redactions, documentaries, screenplays and short stories. He currently lives with his wife in Sydney Australia.

Also by the author and available
from Fileata Fiction

King's Road
Katie
Desire
Chatter